THE WALKING COAT

STORY BY PAULINE WATSON

PICTURES BY TOMIE DE PAOLA

Aladdin Paperbacks

For M.C. from P.W.
For Nancy C. from T. deP.

First Aladdin Paperbacks edition October 1995,
by arrangement with the Walker Publishing Company, Inc.
Text copyright © 1980 by Pauline Watson
Illustrations copyright © by Tomie dePaola

Aladdin Paperbacks
An imprint of Simon & Schuster
Children's Publishing Division
1230 Avenue of the Americas
New York, NY 10020

10 9 8 7 6 5 4 3 2 1

The Library of Congress has cataloged the hardcover edition as follows:
Watson, Pauline.
The walking coat.
Summary: The first time he wears Cousin Charley's
discarded winter coat, Scott finds himself involved in several
interesting situations.
[1. Clothing and dress—Fiction]
I. dePaola, Tomie, ill.   II. Title.
PZ7.W3285Wal   1981   [E]   81-7395
ISBN 0-13-944314-2
ISBN 0-689-80420-2 (Aladdin pbk.)

Reprinted by arrangement with Aladdin Paperbacks,
an imprint of Simon & Schuster Children's Publishing Division.

When Cousin Charley bought himself a new hunting coat,
Scott asked if he might have his old one.
   "Sure," said Cousin Charley.

The coat was brown with green splotches. It had a hood. Scott loved it.

"What in the world will you do with that big heavy coat?" his mother asked.

"I will wear it when winter comes," Scott said. And he hung the coat in his closet.

Some weeks later, in November, Scott went into the front yard. The icy wind whipped around him like a racing car. It was a very cold day.

His eyes became leaking faucets. His nose and fingers felt like icicles. Scott hugged his arms and shivered. Then he remembered Cousin Charley's coat.

He ran to his room, took the coat from the closet, and put it on—hood and all. He went to the mirror and peeked at himself through a hole in the hood. Cousin Charley's coat covered him—*completely*—except for his shoes.

The fur lining was warm. It felt cozy. Now he was ready to go back outside.

Scott walked slowly. He flapped his arms about to keep from bumping into things.

In the yard he giggled. The cold wind could not find him now. He felt snug inside the coat.

It was a good day to go to the park.
"Look! There goes a coat!" someone shouted.
"It's walking! All by itself!" another voice cried.
It was Cindy and Susan.

Scott waved.
"Oh! It sees us!" Cindy shouted.
"Run for your life!" cried Susan.
Scott laughed.

"Hello there, Coat," a friendly voice said behind him. "I'm going to the bakery. Would you like to come with me?"

The voice belonged to his neighbor, Mrs. Capo.

Scott nodded. He felt Mrs. Capo take his coat sleeve.

"Look at that, will you?" a man's voice said. "A lady walking a coat. What next?"

Inside the shop, Mrs. Capo said, "Good morning, Mr. Bobbin. I would like one dozen rolls, please. And a doughnut for this fine looking coat."

"A doughnut for a coat! A coat that eats doughnuts?" Mr. Bobbin's voice was loud with surprise. "Are you sure?"

"Of course, I'm sure," said Mrs. Capo. "Say, Coat," she asked, "do you want your doughnut glazed?"

Scott shook his head.

"A . . . mazzzz . . . ing," Mr. Bobbin said.

Scott felt something soft and sugary at his fingertips. It was the doughnut.

He took it and guided the long coat sleeve under the hood to his mouth.

Then he took a bite.

"Unbelievable!" exclaimed Mr. Bobbin. "I have never seen anything like it. Here, Sleeve," he said, "have another."

Scott took the doughnut at the fingertips of his right hand.

"Thank you," he said.

"It talks!" cried Mr. Bobbin.

"It's a smart coat," said Mrs. Capo. "Polite, too."

"A . . . mazzzz . . . ing," said Mr. Bobbin.

When Scott left the bakery, he started toward the park.

"Hey, Coat! Look this way! I want your picture for *The Evening Star!*"

Scott turned and the voice called out, "Thanks! See you in the news!"

In the park, Scott sat down to rest. Soon he would look for his friend Ray.

"Oh! You see the strangest creatures in the park these days," he heard someone complain.

"How unsafe!" said another.

Scott looked around. But he did not see the creature. Instead he saw two people hurrying away.

He walked around a large statue to look for Ray. He saw a small dog. He warmed it under his coat until the owner came looking for it.

Someone screamed: "HELP! A thief!"

Scott had never seen a thief. He ran to look. He ran CRASH right into him!

A policeman came running. "Thank you, Coat," he said. "That was quick thinking."

Ray was leaving the park when Scott found him.
"Where did you get that coat?" he asked.
"From Cousin Charley," Scott said.
"I wish I had one like that," said Ray.

Scott unbuttoned the front. "Get in," he said, "I will walk you home."

"My word!" said a loud voice as the boys walked slowly along. "A walking coat!"

"A four-footed coat!" a small voice cried.

Scott and Ray giggled.

"Look at that! A walking, giggling, four-footed coat!" someone else said.

Horns honked. Voices laughed. And hands clapped.

Scott was happy and hungry for lunch when he returned to his own house.

He went into the kitchen to find his mother.

"Help!" she cried. "A robber!"

Scott removed the hood from his face. His eyes sparkled.
"It's not a robber," he said. "IT'S ME!"